Dear Parents:

Congratulations! Your child is taking the first steps on an exciting journey. The destination? Independent reading!

STEP INTO READING® will help your child get there. The program offers five steps to reading success. Each step includes fun stories and colorful art or photographs. In addition to original fiction and books with favorite characters, there are Step into Reading Non-Fiction Readers, Phonics Readers and Boxed Sets, Sticker Readers, and Comic Readers—a complete literacy program with something to interest every child.

Learning to Read, Step by Step!

Ready to Read   Preschool–Kindergarten
• big type and easy words • rhyme and rhythm • picture clues
For children who know the alphabet and are eager to begin reading.

Reading with Help   Preschool–Grade 1
• basic vocabulary • short sentences • simple stories
For children who recognize familiar words and sound out new words with help.

Reading on Your Own   Grades 1–3
• engaging characters • easy-to-follow plots • popular topics
For children who are ready to read on their own.

Reading Paragraphs   Grades 2–3
• challenging vocabulary • short paragraphs • exciting stories
For newly independent readers who read simple sentences with confidence.

Ready for Chapters   Grades 2–4
• chapters • longer paragraphs • full-color art
For children who want to take the plunge into chapter books but still like colorful pictures.

STEP INTO READING® is designed to give every child a successful reading experience. The grade levels are only guides; children will progress through the steps at their own speed, developing confidence in their reading.

Remember, a lifetime love of reading starts with a single step!

Copyright © 2016 Disney Enterprises, Inc. All rights reserved. Published in the United States by Random House Children's Books, a division of Penguin Random House LLC, 1745 Broadway, New York, NY 10019, and in Canada by Random House of Canada, a division of Penguin Random House Ltd., Toronto, in conjunction with Disney Enterprises, Inc.

Step into Reading, Random House, and the Random House colophon are registered trademarks of Penguin Random House LLC.

Visit us on the Web!
StepIntoReading.com
randomhousekids.com

Educators and librarians, for a variety of teaching tools, visit us at RHTeachersLibrarians.com

ISBN 978-0-7364-3454-6 (trade) — ISBN 978-0-7364-8208-0 (lib. bdg.) — ISBN 978-0-7364-3455-3 (ebook)

Printed in the United States of America
10 9 8 7 6 5 4 3 2 1

Disney

ZOOTOPIA

SUPER ANIMALS!

By Rico Green

Illustrated by the Disney Storybook Art Team

Random House 🏠 New York

Judy Hopps is a bunny.
Bunnies have
great eyesight.
Judy sees the city of
Zootopia all around her.

Judy hears

the smallest sounds.

This helps her do her job.

Judy has strong legs.
She can run fast
and jump high.
Her legs help her
catch criminals.

Nick Wilde is a fox.

Foxes run fast!

Nick has a friend
named Finnick.

Finnick is a fennec fox.
Fennec foxes have
big ears.

Their ears help
keep them cool.

Fru Fru is a shrew.
Shrews have a great sense
of smell . . . and style.

Mr. Big is Fru Fru's dad.

He has good hearing.

But sometimes
he does not listen.

Flash is a sloth.
To save energy,
sloths move
very, very slowly.

Mr. Manchas is a jaguar.
Jaguars have very
sharp teeth . . .
for smiling.

Chief Bogo is
a Cape buffalo.
Cape buffaloes
are very strong.
Bogo is
Judy's boss.

Bellwether is a sheep.

Sheep have

excellent memories.

Bellwether uses
her memory
to help Nick and Judy
solve a case.

Nick has great
night vision.
He can see
in the dark.

Night vision helps Nick
escape from dark places.
He shows Judy
which way to go.

Mayor Lionheart is a lion.

Lions have loud roars.

They can be heard

across Zootopia.

A male lion grows
a big mane.

All the animals
in Zootopia
are super!

ARCTIC SHREW

Mr. Big

REAL ANIMAL FACTS

- Bad eyesight
- Has to eat every five hours
- Excellent hearing

GOAT

REAL ANIMAL FACTS

- Great vision
- Will eat anything
- Very curious and smart

YAK

Yax

REAL ANIMAL FACTS

- Very friendly
- Soft fur
- Likes living in colder areas

CAPE BUFFALO

Chief Bogo

REAL ANIMAL FACTS

- Big and strong
- Likes to herd other animals
- Horns strong enough to stop a bullet

Disney
ZOOTOPIA

GOAT

Disney
ZOOTOPIA

ARCTIC SHREW

Mr. Big

Disney
ZOOTOPIA

CAPE BUFFALO

Chief Bogo

Disney
ZOOTOPIA

YAK

Yax